MAMMA DECEMBA

MAMMA DECEMBA

NIGEL D. MOFFATT

faber and faber
LONDON · BOSTON

First published in 1987
by Faber and Faber Limited
3 Queen Square London WC1N 3AU

Photoset by Wilmaset Birkenhead Wirral
Printed in Great Britain by
Redwood Burn Ltd Trowbridge Wiltshire
All rights reserved

British Library Cataloguing in Publication Data

Moffatt, Nigel D.
Mamma Decemba.
I. Title
822'.914   PR6063.04/
ISBN 0–571–14775–5

CHARACTERS

MAMMA DECEMBA
MERTEL – a close friend
JOHN – MAMMA's husband

Mamma Decemba was first performed by the Temba Theatre Company in association with Birmingham Repertory on 14 November 1985 at the Birmingham Rep Studio. The cast was as follows:

MAMMA DECEMBA	Elizabeth Clarke
MERTEL	Claire Benedict
JOHN	Bill Glasgow
Director	Alby James
Designer	Clarinda Salandy
Lighting Designer	Paul Armstrong

ACT ONE

SCENE ONE

MAMMA DECEMBA *is sitting in her living-room in an old rocking-chair. In the centre of the room is a dining-table surrounded by three chairs. To the right of the room is a large settee. Her head is wrapped with a scarf, the top of her hair showing a silvery grey. On the back wall are pictures of 'The Last Supper', one of Christ and a framed picture of Prince Charles and Princess Diana next to them. There is a small table below them, on which lies a telephone. At sixty-two years of age she has been made redundant; three months ago she lost her husband.*

MAMMA D: It-a rain. Don't look like we goin' to have much snow dis year. Tip tap, tip tap, all de time a jus' so it go on. Rain, rain, rain. I wonder where me husband is now? A-sleep . . . a-sleep. Twenty-seven years . . . and for what? For what? To bury him on English soil? Jamaica! Jamaica! Lord! What we come here for? What did possess we to come to dis hell-forsaken place? We coulda live; we coulda feed and clothes we children them: what make we come-a England? (*She wipes her right eye.*) Work all your life for children . . . and what you get? 'Me have me husband to look after.' The next one have her children them to look after. The boy children them don't have no time, sa! Them gone to chase after white woman frock-tail. The bitch them! Them goin' to get all them-a buck for . . . you mark me word. Them father come-a England with a dream, a dream of workin' together, savin' we money, then goin' back home to start one steady business. A little shop woulda do; a little taxi business woulda suffice . . . him wasn't a fussy man. No sooner come here – save to send for children them – and we-a save again! them a get married. One in love, the other one pregnant. Bless me soul, boy! You ever hear anything like-a this? Now the boy children them a come tell me me come from Africa. Jesus! Me know you comin' for

3

your World, Lord! Me know . . . you're comin', Lord! (*She stretches out her hands for a moment*) Bless me, poor husband, dead and gone. Three months . . . that's all! Three months and them don't expec' me to still a cry. Only Jesus know how I miss him! How I miss him. Jesus! Help me to keep me way clean that me might see him face in heaven. May my heart be pure, Almighty Father. (*She begins to rock in the chair.*) Lord, you know it hard. Them all too busy to come see me . . . busy hatchin' up heap-a picny for the Government to pay to feed! No wonder the English want them out-a them blasted country. We come here, we work, we never ask nobody for nothin'; never owe nobody a single penny: we skimp and scrape till we coulda buy what we want. Lord know it was never easy. Come here, find that we have to live like-a dogs in Indian man house: how them coulda hark and spit in the sink and on the floor . . . Lord, me wi' never know. Make you stomach sick when you have to go in-a them kitchen to cook. The bitch them was nasty. John workin' eight till five, five days a week and half day Saturday, all for five poun' two shillin' a week. Them times me wasn't workin'. When me come here and see what him bring me to, me bawl! Me bawl and me bawl and me bawl! Cryin' say me want to go home, me miss me mumma and me picny them. Then me buck me foot. Find a job in-a one factory . . . pay me four poun' three shillin' a week . . . me glad! Me say, me glad! Lord know how me was glad. Me send money a week time for Mumm, for the children them, and we still manage to throw two hand a partner* a week, till we coulda send for the picny them. (*She stops the chair rocking.*) In no time after sendin' for them, we buy a house. Them don't want no blacks here so, them don't want no blacks there so. Till we buck luck and en'-up with this. It wasn't what me did

---

two hand a partner: this refers to weekly payments of £5 by a group of people to an individual (one hand of partner). Thus 'two hand a partner' is double this payment.

4

want, but at least it was a roof over we head. Now you tell me what John work all him life for? To give everything to these tomboys them, so them can go out and fling it away 'pon English woman? Me work for them all me life and me know what me did have to put-up with under them: and them not gettin' a fart of what me and my husband work for. Blas' them. (*She rocks in the chair.*) Say them left home, gone to live with gal, yet every so of-ten you see them a come man: 'Mamma, you cook? Me hungry.' You tell me, them not eatin' where them live? Them woman not feedin' them? Then what the hell them doin' with them then? If it was Jamaica and a woman stay so, man wouldn't even spit 'pon her whatless live with her . . . him woulda kick her arse out-a the house! You think them pa woulda put up with it? Not one of them come like-a him. God bless him. Now and again me might see me grand-children them – when them not too busy to come see me. This-ya generation different from my generation, by a long way. Every day Mumm used to see my picny them; me make it me point of duty to send them to see them grandmother. Today, them don't care: me old and them young; them a English and me a Jamaican; them have education and me don't have none. Me can't understan' their way of life, you see. Me dumb, them clever. Pissin' idiot them! Them husband spend off all them pissin' money and a them same one have to go to work every day to pay off for brand new car – and them can't drive; to pay off for them hell-ever mortgage, for them hell-ever house. Must have the best, man! Boy, you don't know my family: the best or nothin'. The bitch them goin' to fart though! Me tell you. Still a rain. Don't look like we goin' to have no snow dis year.
(*Blackout.*)

The scenery remains the same. MAMMA DECEMBA *still rocking in the rocking-chair. 'How great thou art' by Burl Ives playing on the cassette recorder. She sings along with it. When it stops the cassette automatically shuts off. She does not move.*

MAMMA D: Sun-a shine. What a beautiful day. Make a change from all the rain of yesterday. If only we was in-a Jamaica now! Pickin' and plantin'! Lord! What a joy it woulda be, ee, John?

(*A blackman dressed in a white suit, gloves, shoes, shirt and tie, enters the room from the left. He stands behind* MAMMA DECEMBA. *He has grey hair and a pallid, deathly, complexion.*)

If me coulda jus' see you one more time.

(*He walks to the other side of the room and exits.*)

What-a handsome man him was. From Westmoreland to Mantego Bay, the gal them did love him, you see! Me was so proud. And how him was so thin again . . . chuh! John was a star boy, man. Him make certain everybody know . . . him have heap a gal, you see. Mumm did say him would never settle down: but him settle down when him buck-up 'pon me. 'You won't keep him! you won't keep him!' But me did know say a fart them was talkin'. Give a man what him think him want, what more him ago ask for? (*She stops the chair.*) Make them back-a-wall people go away from me, yaa! When them a comb lice out-a them picny head, mine them at school. Make them go away from me. (*She rocks the chair.*) Three months, and every day me see less and less somebody. What do me? Me not human? (*She stops rocking the chair.*) Me don't need to talk to somebody like everybody else!? When you old them don't want to know you! Less them have trouble a them yard, or them want money. Not that you have it, but you have to find it to give them. You see, them don't care if you live or dead. Piss to them! Why we shoulda come a England, work we backside

6

off, just to leave it all to them? Make them come kiss me arse! Me a what? (*She starts rocking in the chair again.*) If them think say me-a cunnu-munnu* for them, them make a big mistake. Black people! Black people! Me will never know what do Jamaicans. We all want the best for we self, and don't give a damn for nobody. How can we live like that, you tell me? We go to Jamaica in Eighty-One: picny them killin' ma and pa. And a the same now in England. Them just a wait till you dead! Then, them a come fight for what them feel left for them. Some a them just a pray for you to dead. (*She laughs.*) Oh, my God! Me can't do better than laugh. One woman, no sooner her husband dead, the eldest son come down from Kingston. Him go up a the house with one piece a bamboo chana† . . . and when him weave it so and weave it so . . . him send the ma and her two boy picny them runnin' like-a fart. Me laugh! When the woman tell me, me couldn't do no better than laugh. Me never think then, say the same thing was goin' to happen to me – or coulda happen to me. But look where me is now. Brother and sister, don't laugh after one another, cause your day a-come. Lord, have mercy 'pon them. (*She stops the chair.*) All me know, my husband was no scab. Him never one day take my money to go to pub for drink! The most him ever do is buy him cigarette – and sometimes some tobacco for him pipe. Me never have to go run find him, just to ask him what him do with his money – after me take mine pay off all the bills them and don't even have penny to go do me shoppin' . . . after me don't fool. And when you go ask them, what else you expect him to say: 'Me don't ask you what you do with your pay packet, so why you a question me for?' What else can you expect? A man is a man and a woman is a woman, no mystery don't in-a that. (*She begins to rock in the chair again.*) The younger

cunnu-munnu: a fool.

†*bamboo chana*: a piece of bamboo, sometimes used as a cricket bat.

7

generation full a joke, sa. The sun still a shine. Spring look like it goin' to be nice this year. At least it stop rain. (*Blackout.*)

SCENE THREE

MERTEL, *a slightly younger woman than* MAMMA DECEMBA, *is sitting at the head of the dinner table to the right of room. She's wearing her coat, it is loose.* MAMMA DECEMBA *rocks in chair.*

MERTEL: Mamma D, why you don't lie down on de settee and try fe get some rest, yu mus' tired.

MAMMA D: Yes, me tired, but wha' use yu tired if you can't sleep?

MERTEL: Even if yu nuh sleep, yu body woulda relax.

MAMMA D: Yu think so?

MERTEL: It as good as a long soak ina de bath – me do it all de time a yard. You want to hear Sam to me now, 'What you a do ina de bathroom, yu sick?' Me now nuh answer him, 'Yu dead in there, or a hear you nuh hear me?' De brute mad, yu see. (*She laughs.*) Him don't change, yu nuh; from Jamaica to ya, him still de same . . . but me wouldn't change him. Him have him ways, but him good to me.

MAMMA D: From mornin'.

MERTEL: Yet yu hear some woman talk, and the way them go on in dis country, you'da think say them can't wait fe them husband dead. Them even make them husband take out insurance policy – mind yu, fe me take out one to – and as soon as them dead, them off man, Miami then Jamaica: turn tourist, yu nuh.

MAMMA D: If them want to go to Jamaica and pop them style a fe them good luck, cause a ask them a ask fe get them backside broke.

MERTEL: A suh me hear! All a them a gun!

MAMMA D: Who say so?

MERTEL: Nuh so me hear.

MAMMA D: Don't make people full yu head with damn
        rubbish, yaa.
MERTEL: Rubbish or nuh rubbish, if me was in de position of
        them deh woman deh, when me reach Miami not even the
        devil himself get me to go any further.
        (*They both laugh.*)
MAMMA D: Gu weh!
MERTEL: We don't know what goin' on over there.
MAMMA D: All me know is dis, bad or good, a me country. Me
        don't have time fe curse where me-a come from.
MERTEL: But what if a true, like what me hear 'bout some
        woman deh obeah them husband – after them nuh manage
        to poison them? Me hear say some a them, a them preacher
        deh help them fe kill off them husband . . . then them
        marry somebody in the congregation . . . me hear say them
        usually gi' the preacher some kinda donation.
        (MAMMA DECEMBA *laughs.*)
MAMMA D: Me never hear so much damn nonsense in all me
        born days.
MERTEL: Me only tell you wha' me hear. Me even hear say dis
        one woman get some kind a medicine that when de husband
        swallow it and it get into him stomach it turn into splinter
        of wood: me hear say it make him shit himself till him
        dead.
        (MAMMA DECEMBA *laughs.*)
        Nyam out the whole a him inside.
MAMMA D: You stay there a make people fool yu. Where you
        get them things from anyway, a make you make them up?
MERTEL: Mamma D, me don't say a thing, not a thing, me jus'
        sit down deh a listen, mindin' me owna business.
        (MAMMA DECEMBA *turns and looks at* MERTEL.)
        (*Blackout.*)

SCENE FOUR

MAMMA DECEMBA *enters the room from the right, carrying four*

9

*plates with an equal number of knives and forks. She sets the
table, then sits in her rocking-chair.*

MAMMA D: Dinner soon cook. Me bet them blasted boys soon
come, them tongue a-hang down like-a dog. Get them good
education, and what them do with it? We never get that.
From me twelve me never go to no school. Work to do . . .
and five mout' to feed . . . Mum did need all the help she
coulda get. Me-a the last one. Couldn' stay at school, so me
left. We make the sacrifice without knowin' what kind of
sacrifice we was makin', till we come to England: and for
everything . . . you have to be able to read and write. From
me twelve till now, me been workin' for other people.
Them have what them call, 'O'level, and them not workin'!
Just livin' off the Government. What is the world comin'
to? Me ask meself. (*She stops the chair from rocking.*) Mertel
was tellin' me the other day say, her son, Steven, who a
twenty-six, goin' out at night to steal car to go to nightclub
– then him steal another one to come back. Police catch
him and police catch him, but still him won't stop. When
him nineteen him come home bout him in love; next thing
them know the boy pick himself up and go marry this white
gal. She was pregnant . . . but-a love him did love her, him
say. Not even six months after him married the gal . . . she
left him. Bam-kitty him in Court for cruelty. The gal say
him used to beat her up and want to put her on the street.
Me ask you, in the name of we Almighty Saviour, how in
God's name that boy coulda want to put a woman – who's
eight months pregnant – on the street? And what worse,
the Court believe her blasted story. Me-a tell you, you can't
trust these blasted white people! No matter how nice and
smiley smiley them is with you. Them sell you like-a fart on
the wind for them own people! Me tell you that now.
Anyway, the boy galang and galang till bad company
befrien' him, and him and them start thieve from people
house. Mertel say ever since him married that gal him head
not for him. Them hardly see them grand-picny, and when

10

it come them say it don't want to go. Mertel said the
mother can't be feedin' the picny properly: nuh the same
thing me little while a-go was sayin'? Now the boy broke-
down to nothin'. Police catch him and him frien' them.
Now it look like him goin' to go to prison. She tell me say
people say she shouldn't go to visit him; but me tell her say
if a it she want to do, she must do it! An' not give a blas'
what them natty head nigger want to say. What you don't
want for you'self don't give to somebody else. Don't matter
how bad them is, a your picny them: nobody did help you
born them. If them to kill, then you kill them. You get old,
don't have nobody, probably a them same one turn you
hand and foot. Me not killin' me picny them for nobody!
Not me! Me, sa? Not this-a same Mamma Decemba. Me
mighta stupid but me not fool. (*She starts rocking the chair.*)
Life hard, but we all a one family, same blood, what me
want to cut me-self and make me-self bleed for? Every day
she go see him now, me hear. Poor Mertel, from me know
that woman she have it hard. Her eldest son, Beris, have
picny in-a every town and city in England! Him beat them;
him cut them up; him send them out 'pon street; till every
year become just another year spend in-a prison. Now the
youngest one look like him a head the same way. Them
don't stay like them pa, though! Him like to gamble, yes,
but that's as far as it go. Mertel is a sweet understandin'
soul, too understandin'. Him goin' to thieve, yes! But him
is not coming to and from my house to go thieve. It woulda
better if him did go out and kill somebody, than say him a-
go thieve. (*She stops the chair rocking.*) What them goin' to
thieve for? You tell me now, what them-a go out go thieve
for? Them get money from the Government; them get
money from we, them parents, all we have to give; them get
them food cook and put 'pon table, however many times
them want it, suh you tell me now, what reason them
have to go out go thieve? Don't it follow that a bad
company them-a follow? It's the English boy and gal them

go to school with them-a follow! Lock up them backside yes! Me don't blame them. (*She turns slowly and looks at the table. She stares for a moment then sighs.*) Haa, sa. (*Then she turns around and begins rocking in the chair once again.*) Looking out-a the same old dirty window from the same old room. One day rain, the next sunshine. No matter which one me bones them still damn cold. (*She stops the chair from rocking, and looks in amazement, on the edge of her seat.*) Watch-ya now! It-a SNOW!! (*Pause.*) Me wonder if Danny and Jammy comin' down today. Them-a go get wet if them come.

(*Blackout.*)

SCENE FIVE

MERTEL *is sitting at the table. Her coat on.* MAMMA DECEMBA *is sitting in the rocking-chair. She is still.*

MERTEL: So yu don't feel no better then, Mamma D?

MAMMA D: Me don't even know what it mean, me dear sista'. Time hard fe all.

MERTEL: Fe some, more than fe others.

MAMMA D: Wha' yu say tru', me can't deny dat.

MERTEL: Everyt'ing come so sudden in-a life, an' when yu t'ink yu safe, somet'ing else come co' knock yu dung. Me try fe understan' it, Mamma D, but de whole damn t'ing frighten de hell out-a me. Me never se' yu like this before.

MAMMA D: Gal, hush yu mout', yaa: yu ever know this happen to me before?

(MERTEL *hangs her head, then looks up.*)

MERTEL: Some t'ings tek time.

MAMMA D: Time . . . time. (*Shakes her head.*) Time gone, an' life empty.

MERTEL: Life full, man, wha' do yu? Tek yu husband pension an' guh 'pon a cruise; tek a long holiday; tek time fe relax

de old body – an' de Lord will tek care of de pain.
Nothin' last forever, yu nuh.

MAMMA D: Not even life.

MERTEL: Woman, wha' yu seh? A fe me grave yu-a try fe dig?

MAMMA D: A de last t'ing deh 'pon fe me mind ya now.

MERTEL: Then yu nuh fe talk dem deh way deh, Mamma D;
unless yu want me fe guh find de nearest railway line?
(MERTEL *laughs slightly.*)

MAMMA D: (*As if receiving a blow to the stomach*) Oh, God! (*She
holds her stomach.*) Help me oh, Lord! Deliver me from de
ways of sin! Oh mighty Saviour! Show me thy road from
sin! I stand a humble sinner before yu, oh Lord! De mark
of Cain res' on yu sinful chil'ren, oh, God! Have mercy on
one pitiful sinner, oh, Almighty Saviour! Thou knowest all
. . . an' I . . . nothin'.
(*Blackout.*)

SCENE SIX

MERTEL *is sitting at the head of the dinner table.* MAMMA
DECEMBA *rocks in the chair.*

MERTEL: Me don't know how you can sit down in-a Deadhouse
so, day after day. You not frighten?

MAMMA D: (*Looks straight ahead all the time*) Frighten of what,
me dear? Me husband? How me can frighten of me own
husband?

MERTEL: If it was me, me gone long time! Me not stayin' in-a
no Deadhouse. If Sam shoulda dead now . . . me get up
and me gone! A one thing me cannot stand.

MAMMA D: How come when John dead me keep him in-a the
house overnight? Me never 'fraid. How me can 'fraida me
own husband? All in the middle of the night me come
downstairs ya, and talk to him. Me not lettin' my dead just

13

pass the door, me sister. If-a here them live them can come in, and if dead have power to use, and can only use it badly, make them come in here and use it. Me can't 'fraid of me own husband, Mertel.

MERTEL: When you did tell me say you was goin' to keep him body overnight before the burial, me never believe you. Me couldn't stay in-a the house ya now . . . me one.

MAMMA D: Him gone now, Mertel, gone. Nothin' we can do 'bout it now. When you time call you can't tell it to wait. Don't believe all of what them damn fool people them tell you: duppy don't have finger to jook out anybody eye. Them say, 'You can take the people out of the country, but you can't take the country out-a the people,' so a them ya now. Them is just ignorant people, Mertel, ignorant people.

(MERTEL *exits right of the room.* MAMMA DECEMBA *unaware of this.*)

MAMMA D: You don't see them comin' from Market Saturday day-time: one hand to carry all them basket, while them have to use the other hand to hold up them arse! You don't see them? Anybody woulda think say them don't have toilet where them walk. (*She stops rocking in the chair.*) When me say me miss him me mean say me miss him! Just because me don't tie-up me head and hold it down 'pon street don't mean say me don't miss him. Me can't just go show everybody! Me can't go and bare me flesh to them, only for them to use it to kill me! Me don't want them to know me business, sister Mertel. John dead, but him will always be with me. Me can never forget him . . . no matter what nobody want to say. Him up there now, a graveyard, under the ground a-sleep. (*She begins to rock in the chair.*) You know, Mertel, at the funeral me see people who me know and faces poor me never behold in me life; but John know all a-them. Black and white alike. A set-up, white Preacher come offer prayer, black Preacher come offer prayer . . . only say the black Preacher pray and sing till mornin' nearly come night again. Rejoice! As him is in Paradise. Wreaths, them come from all over, me couldn't begin to tell you who, where or when. Nine-Night again! Them come. The house full till it overflowin'. People bring food, bring drink . . . so that most of the food spoil and the drinks them over there in the cubby-hole. Forty-Night, the same thing again. When them curry the goat you see man . . . me say, it sweet! And like how we keep back two bottle a-the white rum . . . me say, the people feel so sweet them never want to go home. Eight o'clock the next mornin' them still-a sing. It was no more than what him deserve, though. Him work for it, and what him never get in life him get in him passin' on. If only him coulda get it when him was still alive. (*She stops rocking the chair*) Why him have to dead for him reap him harvest? John! God bless you!

(*He enters the room from the left, still in all white.*)

JOHN: You call me? A me hunnu want?

MAMMA D: (*Hands upheld*) If the dead coulda talk, you woulda speak to me now.

(*He stands in the centre of the room.*)

JOHN: So me is here! What you want me for, woman?

MAMMA D: If me coulda just see him one more time. (*She places her hands in her lap. She speaks softly, on the verge of tears.*) A life, Mertel, a life. Same way we come, same way we have to go. Me know him is in the hands of the Lord. But God knows me miss him! Lord know me did love him! And if a sin me-a sin, cause the Bible say it should be a time-a rejoicin', me beg God to look in-a me heart and see say a not sin me-a sin wilfully, and to forgive me poor sinner. A only because me love him. And not even you picny can understand them things. (*She rocks in the chair.*)

JOHN: (*Stretches out his hands to her*) Every man must know his own burden! Lef' them! Make them live them own life! (*Hands down.*) Yu not livin' your own? Nobody coulda stop you.

MAMMA D: Me father dead; me mother dead; me one brother

15

dead – the other one lame a-dead in-a Jamaica. One sister
in Canada; the other one round the corner a-dead a high
blood pressure and diabetes: her heart could give way at
any time. Me best friend, who me grow up with, dead three
years this year. Now me husband gone to'. Me is alone.
(*She stops the chair rocking.*) When me-a leave Jamaica to
come-a England, me make sure me get somebody
responsible to look after Mumm. Me come here, work,
send money to her, and to the woman who was lookin' after
her. Me never run and say me goin' to live me own life: my
mother is my responsibility! If the other picny them don't
want to help her, that's their business! Me have to play fe
me part . . . to hell with them. No man coulda stop me
from lookin' after me ma! where me sendin' my money is
my business . . . me not askin' him where him sendin' fe
him. Me sa! Me? Them coulda pretty till pretty comin' out
them backside . . . them not stoppin' me from lookin' after
fe me mumma. Make them go shit! The day you dead them
take some floosy come nyam down half of what you live
and work for. Me don't want nobody dead-lef', so me don't
see what make me shoulda give 'way mine.

JOHN: (*He walks over to her and holds the back of the chair*) You
shoulda know better! You of all people shoulda know
better. You don't lef' Mumm back in-a Jamaica? You
brother them go where them want; you sister them go
where them want. Hunnu★ picny them what hunnu lef'
with her to look after . . . as soon as hunnu reach where
hunnu wanted to go, and save hunnu two penny, hunnu
send for hunnu picny them. Lef' hunnu Mumma 'pon her
own. (*He steps back from her chair.*) A what kinda hypocrite
hunnu is? (*He exits left of room.* MAMMA DECEMBA *starts
rocking in her chair.*)

MAMMA D: Yes, me did look after my mother. But you know,
Mertel, things change, people change: it don't stay like

*hunnu: refers to the individual and an associated group at the same time.

16

when we was young. All that gone now. The Lord comin'
for him World. This-ya time it goin' to be fire and
brimstone. Not even one of the wicked goin' to stand. (*She
stops rocking the chair.*) Praise be! We Saviour comin',
Mertel! (*She looks round.*) Mertel?
(*Blackout.*)

ACT TWO

Only the sound of the telephone ringing can be heard. MAMMA
DECEMBA *enters from the right of the room. She is wearing a coat,
gloves, scarf and a little hat. She hurries to answer the phone,
keeping the receiver two to three inches from her.*

MAMMA D: Hello, who is that speakin', please? (JOHN *enters
from left of the room and sits in the rocking-chair.*) Yes, oh yes.
Yes. Yes. Yes. (*In a low voice.*) Tryin' to keep up, you see,
but it not so easy. Oh, yes! We have to count we blessin's.
Not too bad, you know. The family them all right, the last
time me see them. Them come and go, you know, you
know how the younger generation stay. One day somebody
will come, another day nobody don't come. All me can do is
pray to the Lord to give me strength. (*She laughs.*) Oh no,
no. A little bit a shoppin' me go do, and when me-a come in
the entry me hear the phone. So a run me runnin' now to
see a who . . . that's why me's a bit out-a breath. Me all
right, man, what do you? When we time come we can't tell
it to wait, yaa me sister. All we can do is to live we life till
the Lord call we home. My dear! Everythin'! Me say
everything! (*Her voice louder as she rocks back and forth, her
hand on her hip.*) Wha' sa! Me say every God livin' thing, a
solicitor. Have to change over the name of the house, you
see: no man, what do you? In them days only the man name
coulda put down 'pon paper as the owner. So now me have
to go through this and go through that, dig up this and dig
up that, to find out all sort a-paper to take down to them.
The heap-a runnin' up and down that me have do since me
husband dead – God bless me soul – me don't know if me
goin' to make it through another day under this-ya
pressure. All right then, me sister, me will see you soon,
anyway. All right then love, thanks for callin'. Yes, yes,
yes. Thanks for callin', you see. See you soon, and say hello

21

to you family for me, you see. All right then. Me have some
food ya to put on fire for meself, and me don't even feel to
eat whatless fe go cook. No, it not so bad; but when a-only
you one you-a cook for it don't give you the feelin' to stand
up over no dutty stove. All right then me dear, see you
later. Walk good, you hear. (*She puts down the phone.*) Some
people don't think say you have anything better to do all
day than sit down and talk to them. (*She takes off her coat
and scarf which she drapes over one of the chairs, then she takes
off her gloves and hat.*) Me better go put on the pot-a bittle,
yaa. (*The chair rocks. As she is about to look away the chair
rocks again.*) A imagine me-a imagine it or what? Me nuh
just see me rocking-chair rock by itself? (*She rubs her eyes.*)
Come on old gal, a mus' tired you tired; all the rushin'
about down town. (*She sits on one of the chairs by the dinner
table, at the head, to the right of the room.*)

JOHN: Boy, woman can chat me son.

MAMMA D: It easy to say take things easy, but another thing to
do it. Doreen married with for her four picny them; Elaine
with for her husband: the two a-them have for them
husband to go home to at night . . . but a who me have?
(*She rubs her forehead then rests her left hand on the table.*)
You fight for them and you fight for them, and what you
get? Damn all. Them and them husband workin' to make
better life for themself . . . them don't care a cock-a-hole
'bout you. Danny and Jammy? Don't even know where
them is from one minute to the next. (*She starts to rub her
hands as if rinsing clothes.*) Me wish to God me coulda wash
me hands a-them. Sell the damn old house and go home.
Me have me house there and acres of land, what me have
over ya to stop for? What here for me? (*She stops and rests
on the table again.*) Me body old and tired now, time it get
some rest. Here every day just payin' gas bills, electric bills,
rates, house insurance, have to skimp and scrape to buy
food . . . out-a thirty-six pound a week. Lord have mercy!
(*She holds her head.*) These people them cruel, sa! (*Leans on*

22

the table.) Thank God we finish pay de mortgage. Me coulda go back home, start up a little shop, in no time me no well away? Get one little boy to work for me.

JOHN: Woman, stop dreamin'! You know you not goin' no where.

MAMMA D: What you say? (*She looks in the direction of the chair*.) John, a you?

JOHN: No, a no me, a somebody else. You damn fool, ee? A me, yes! Who else? You not goin' any where lef' you picny them. Why you don't let go a-them and lef' them to live them own-a life? You don't live for you? Let them live for them.

MAMMA D: Me can see you clear as day! You come back to me?

JOHN: Can you own life? Look how long me did deh 'pon you for we go home . . . look how long! You never want to know. How come you want to go now?

MAMMA D: But John, how was we to go? We don't know nobody out there. Everybody dead long time. What if somethin' did happen . . . what we woulda do? Nobody to run to; nobody to call upon for a bit-a water; what we woulda do?

JOHN: What did we do before?

MAMMA D: We was young, then.

JOHN: What fe we parents did do?

MAMMA D: Them did have we.

JOHN: What about when we did come away?

MAMMA D: We left somebody to look after them.

JOHN: Then you have the answer to you question . . . hire a house-keeper.

MAMMA D: Me don't want no stranger ina me house!

JOHN: Then what make you think them did want stranger ina them house?

MAMMA D: Me don't know. Me never think it me business fe ask you. Me know how much me look after Mumm. Me over here, me send money . . . when it's not money a clothes . . . me even go out there go see her before she dead.

JOHN: You do her a great favour, so it sounds. You time – not money, is the greatest thing you can give in life. You can't buy or sell kindness. You go out there go see her before she dead . . . what-a favour you do her. Did she ever one day yet, make you feel guilty, sayin' you did leave her? No, not one day she complain in letter or by mouth, when you go out there. So why condemn you own children because them want the same thing?

MAMMA D: But them have what them want already.

JOHN: What the rock-stone we did come ya for then? We never have all we want already, to'? Greed, woman, greed. We suffer from it, and them-a suffer from it now. When them finger burn ina fire, them will realize. Look 'pon you! look how many times you pissin' finger burn ina fire . . . and you don't realize fart.

MAMMA D: Lef' me! Lef' me backside! If a come you come to tell me off, you can . . . piss off! To hell with you! Go kiss me arse.

JOHN: Call hunnu-self Christian?

(*He stands, walks to the side of the chair, taps it so that it rocks by itself. He exits left of room.* MAMMA DECEMBA *looks to her right then looks back again.*)

MAMMA D: What a good thing me never spread out them few piece a clothes me did beat out this mornin'. Rain a fall like nobody business. The forecast did say rain though, that's why me never put them out there to dry.

(*Blackout.*)

SCENE TWO

MAMMA DECEMBA *is sitting in the same chair.* MERTEL *is sitting on the opposite side of the table. Both are looking straight ahead . . . not facing each other.*

MAMMA D: Where's Sam? Gone-a work?

MERTEL: Yes. A days him-a work 'pon this week.

24

MAMMA D: How Steven? You still goin' to see him?

MERTEL: Me take you advice . . . me go see him, poor boy. Him say when the policeman them take him in them give him some kinda beatin', him say him never know say him woulda live. Say him don't care if them want to send him a prison. The boy mad! You see? Ever since that little gal mash him up, him never recover. Sam don't want to know him! Don't want a thing to do with him. Say him wash him hand of him.

MAMMA D: Don't make no man make you turn you back on you picny, you hear? Any time, them can pick up themself, the next thing you know them gone lef' you for some little gal 'pon the streets. Then what you have? Nuh you picny them? Only them you have to look after you. Don't make no man come between you and you picny them, yaa. Make them go fart.

(MERTEL *laughs*.)

MERTEL: Mamma D, you don't make fun.

MAMMA D: Damn and blast to them! Them-a wha'? Woman, go see you picny, yaa. Make the man them go to hell.

MERTEL: Me not goin' to stop from see him. No, sa. Sam only say so, but him don't mean it. Him is as worried as me ya. A so blackman stay from mornin', anyway. How your two them?

MAMMA D: If them ina trouble me don't know, and if them don't ina trouble me don't know. If them don't want to come look for me, what them expect say, me goin' to ride round on bicycle askin' people me don't know for directions, so me can find me owna son, them? Well, if a me them a count 'pon to do that . . . them can stay there a-wait. You never know, them might just get what them-a buck for.

(*Blackout.*)

MAMMA DECEMBA *stands and walks over to the rocking-chair. She sits down and begins to rock slowly in it.*

MAMMA D: Come-a England, work hard to find, life hard to find. So me work a-so me cry. Me never want to stop ya. We never plan to stop ya. But who can know God's plan? Out-a five pound a week me save, John save, till we could afford to buy we owna house. The two boys them come along, set we back, but we fight on. Me manage to go a Jamaica four times since me come ya. First time me go, me was just in time to see Mumm before she dead. Dead ina fire. She was tryin' to see if she coulda cook, and forget all about the pot what was on the fire, when the whole house catch a-blaze. Before them know it, the whole house burn down, and Mumm was nothin' but ashes. (*She stops rocking the chair.*) If only me was there, it wouldn't have happen. God knows how many times it go through me brain. Guilty, Your Honour. But what can me do? Me can't bring her back. One by one me family drop dead over there. Old age? Me don't know. John dead. Sudden heart-attack. Him did want to go back. What was we goin' to go back to? We was fool, though. All we life we save with Barclays Bank, then we decide say we money woulda safer ina Jamaica. Now me dear, bam-kitty! New law: the money can't come back a England if we want it. It devalue so much it woulda worth almost nothin'. Maybe John was right after all, we shoulda gone back home. At least him woulda have a good time after him retirement ina him own country. Him body could be lyin' ina him owna soil, instead a lyin' in the cold, English dutty. And if the rest of the family go home, we goin' to have to lef' him body ya. (*She shakes her head.*) Me thought me was right, but me was wrong. (*She starts rocking in the chair.*) Me make all the wrong decisions. Guilty, Your Honour.

(*Blackout.*)

MAMMA DECEMBA *is asleep in the rocking-chair.* JOHN *enters from left of the room. He walks into the centre of the room.*

JOHN: She's bleedin' again. A different kinda bleedin' this time. She survive these harsh months well, but now the fever of guilt is burnin'. She shed so much tears over me – now she don't have none lef'. Guilt become available, you see. Whenever you need it, you can guarantee it won't let you down. When she hear me cryin' in the ambulance, in the hospital, she don't cry, but she bawl. Me tell her not to worry . . . but she-a born worrier. When she see me dead face she drop, the nurses had to pick her up. She bear up well through it. She was strong at the funeral, so that she surprise many people. British law and bureaucracy keep her busy till now. People rally round her, as is we custom. Now she-a bleed with guilt and remorse. She say what she say, but she don't believe what she-a say, she don't know wha' she-a say. And she too proud, too strong, to ask for help. If she coulda dis go out and meet people, talk to them, listen to them. But no, not Mamma Decemba, boy. She too busy makin' me the man me was not. Me was human as any other human. Just another man passin' through. Love me for what me was! Not what you want me to be. Dis same torch been burnin' too long, Mamma, time we put it out and release the young from dis self-doubtin' ordeal. (*He walks over to her chair and stands behind it.*) A one time me go back a Jamaica – me never recognize the place or people them as bein' Jamaicans. But me woulda live there, cause a there me come from. Woman, if you could only see how things was.

(*Blackout.*)

27

JOHN *goes and lies down on the settee.* MAMMA DECEMBA *wakes suddenly.*

MAMMA D: John, a sleep you was sleepin'?

JOHN: Me must have drop' off for a second.

MAMMA D: Me suppose you don't clean off the chicken for tomorrow's dinner? And the meat me lef' 'pon fire! (*She stands and quickly runs out to the right of the room.*) Thank God! You lucky, it don't burn up. You woulda out of a dinner tonight, let me tell you.

JOHN: Woman, you worry up you'self too much. Why you don't calm you'self?

MAMMA D: How me fe calm meself when me have a lazy bitch like-a you around me? (*She re-enters to sit next to the table.*) Dis mornin' me get up, me wash out you dutty clothes them and hang them out 'pon the line, as the day did look nice. Then, me straight down town to do the shoppin', when you up ya havin' you breakfast. Me one have to carry the hell-ever heavy bag them! While you sit down 'pon you backside watchin' horse racin' 'pon television. Me come home, me make tea for me and you, make sandwich for you nyam again, then me wash up the two lots of dutty things them and put the meat on the fire to cook. Me start watch one programme on the television and ask you to watch the meat so it don't burn, and what you do? Fall a blasted sleep. A what kinda tu-fengae* man, you?

JOHN: A you was sleepin', you know, not me.

MAMMA D: You favour jack-arse.

JOHN: Then me don't know what you favour.

MAMMA D: You shoulda know, you have long enough to find out.

JOHN: Who say me want to know? You see you face favour mongoose.

tu-fengae: no good

MAMMA D: You must like it though, to stop so long.

JOHN: You wash and iron me dutty clothes and cook me food, what me have to complain over?

MAMMA D: You's a facety bitch! You see how you lip kin-up like-a monkey backside?

JOHN: As long as it don't kin-up like-a fe you.

MAMMA D: And people think say you-a somebody.

JOHN: And them don't think of you a blast! (*He laughs.*)

MAMMA D: Me don't go to people house purpose for them to know me business, so them can broadcast it. Me not one a-them back-a-wall people them. Me don't mix with them riff-raff, you is enough for me.

JOHN: But wait! A who dis a talk? Me never know say you a Queen Victoria, gal? Fart, me married to you all this time and me never know say me was royalty. How come you never ask you own husband to lunch at Buckingham Palace? Woman, kiss out me wish-eh-part! And lef' me backside make fly take it.

MAMMA D: Maybe if you did wash it now and again maggidge wouldn't be diggin' a hole in you arse.

JOHN: If you know say it not gettin' wash why you don't take soap and water and come wash it for me? Even Prince Charles have to wash him backside, you know. But me always think say a somebody else do it for him, maybe a you, as you is him mother.

MAMMA D: For a man you can mout', sa.

JOHN: If me couldn't, me woulda fart with you.

MAMMA D: Man, stop the damn noise a me head! You-a give me headache.

JOHN: Somebody always a give you headache. Me feel a bit tired, you know.

MAMMA D: A so? Why you don't curl up on the settee and go sleep?

JOHN: (*He does so*) Wake me when the dinner cook.

MAMMA D: Me will wake you, you go sleep.
  (*Blackout.*)

29

MAMMA DECEMBA *is sitting in the rocking-chair.*

MAMMA D: It-a rain. Me wonder if summer goin' to be hot dis
year. Last year we have a good few days a it – but it never
last. Always a rain in England. Mind you, me can't take the
heat like how me used to. When me go back-a Jamaica it
nearly kill me stiff dead! The sun burn me, you see. Yet,
when John did go back the one and only time, it never
touch him at all. The people them out there say him-a real
Jamaican, just like him never lef' there. Ha, John, me
wonder where you is now. (*She stops rocking.*) Twenty-seven
years him work for British Rail, only to end up with a clock
and a certificate to hang 'pon the wall. No grand pay-off. A
nice little party with all him mates and gaffer singin' him
praises. What a tribute! What a tribute! Different from the
days when them was callin' him 'Black Bastard' do this, do
that. Long way from when them did want to beat him up,
because them did think say them was workin' harder than
him, but him was gettin' bigger pay-packet. This one
whiteman was on to him every day! Till John take it, till
John take it, till him could take no more. Him grab the
man by him shirt collar, pick him up into the air, and tell
him say if him don't take him smell off him back, him goin'
break every bone ina fe him body. Him behave him
backside from that day on, though. Little bit after we hear
say them sack the man. Me spend me life ina factory. Work
me life away 'pon dutty big machine. A night, when me
come home, me hand them full a metal. Me have to take
pin pick them out one by one. Sometimes me come home,
me two hands them ina splaster. Because the bitch them see
say you black, them work you out 'pon the biggest
machines with the heaviest and the hardest of the work.
Earn while you work, sister, earn what you work. When the
bitch them see say you can do the job better and faster than
the white woman them, the foreman befriend you, the other

30

women take hatred of you, say you earning more money
than them. Work go scarce, you become the last person the
foreman wants to know . . . can't afford you. Them can't
afford to make you redundant, so them make you life hell.
UNION? Them don't worth the name. When me get me
accident at work, them never want to know 'bout
representin' me. Although the accident take place at work
and a one of the management have to bring me home.
Them never want to know. But when them was goin' on fe
them strike, poor me never know what them strikin' about,
but me was out there with them, bout me's on strike.
Where did all that UNION money go? What happen to the
money we pay into it? Me end up not gettin' a blasted
penny. So many years, and for what? When them did need
people to work hard, them call black people them only
friend, cause them own people too damn lazy. Now them
don't have no work, we out-a job, and them-a call we
'SPONGERS' off them Government. Them fool we, but
them don't fool we picny them. (*She starts rocking in the
chair again.*) Life so depressin' nowadays. Even the weather
depressin'. 'Rain a fall but dutty tough'; So old time people
used to say.

JOHN: (*From outside*) Mamma D!!!

MAMMA D: (*She looks back suddenly, one hand clutching her heart*)
John!
(*Blackout.*)

SCENE SEVEN

MERTEL *is sitting at the head of the dinner table, her coat on, but
unbuttoned.* MAMMA DECEMBA *is sitting in the rocking-chair.*

MERTEL: Dead. Me nuh like hear bout dead, you nuh. Me nuh
even walk under ladder. People can say what them want
. . . everybody 'fraid o'something or other. When my
mother take sick and a dead a me sister have to come from

Kingston to Savanna-la-mar to look after har . . . me gone. Nuh because me never want to look after har, but blood and sickness a two things me can't stand. A then me meet me first husband. Three years, three picny. Him beat me till me couldn't talk . . . then him lef' me fe one woman a Kingston. A market me first meet John and through him me buck 'pon Sam . . . well, yu know all that a'ready. Mamma D, a time fe yu enjoy yu life now, yu nuh. You can't carry on forever so . . . you just goin' to kill yu-self, and yu know say a nuh that John woulda want. Him was a strong man, now yu have to strong to'! Him dead, and nothin' yu goin' to do can bring him back. Look 'pon yu children and grandchildren . . . yu have a lovely family! You luckier than most. Me now can't rest from one day to the next cause-a worry over wha' mine them goin' to do next . . . and you know Sam long wash him hands of them . . . everywhere – up an' dung – a me one. When Steven nuh lock up, him never make it him duty fe once in awhile come-a yard . . . him after gal! Gal mad! One a these days them goin' to give him some kind-a disease that no matter where him go, everybody can see it, how it broke out 'pon him face. That's if him nuh go a prison. What must I do, Mamma D, what must I do? Yu owna pain hide yu from mine, and yu, me reliable shoulder. And me can't help you. Tell 'tory, keep company, me know you's in another world. Only de Almighty can help you now. Dead. Yu don't know how me hate de sound of de wo'd. Every time me first husband hit me, me did feel say me gwi' dead. You only think so, Mamma D. You only think so, Mamma D. (*She stands and goes to exit right of stage, buttoning her coat.*) You only think so, Mamma D.
(*Blackout.*)

MAMMA DECEMBA *is still sitting in the rocking-chair.* JOHN *enters the room from the left and sits on the chair at the head of the table – to the right.*

JOHN: Me come.

MAMMA D: (*Looks straight ahead*) You come for me?

JOHN: You call me, so me come.

MAMMA D: But you not goin' to come again?

JOHN: No. You know that.

MAMMA D: So you come for me? Will it hurt, John?

JOHN: What hurt is what you make hurt. Me is at peace where me is. Me dream to the rest of the family for them to tell you . . . them don't tell you?

MAMMA D: Yes – me will find peace to', with you?

JOHN: But me never dream to you because me did know, for you, me would have to come back.

MAMMA D: Come back to fetch me?

JOHN: To make you belief stronger. Ease you spirit so it float.

MAMMA D: Me goin' to dead! Me goin' to dead! Me goin' to dead!! (*Holds her head.*)

JOHN: Be at peace. Rest now. Consider Christ we Saviour, in you dreams and in you workin'. Be at peace with the world. Be at peace with you-self. Make guilt and hatred leave you soul! Set you spirit free!

(MAMMA DECEMBA *is lying to one side of the chair, eyes closed.*)

John is at peace. John is happy where him is. Burden yourself and others no more. John is at peace. (*He walks slowly to exit left of the room.*) John is at peace. John is happy where him is.

(*He exits.* MERTEL *enters from the right. She sees* MAMMA DECEMBA *and rushes over to her.*)

MERTEL: Mamma D, wake up! Wake up! (*She shakes her.* MAMMA DECEMBA *opens her eyes. She then rubs them.*) Me did think say . . .

33

MAMMA D: Me must have fallen asleep. Me have a strange dream. Me was talkin' to John and him was talkin' to me as if him wasn't dead . . . but alive. (*She looks behind her.*)

MERTEL: What you lookin' for?

MAMMA D: Nothin'. Gone dis time. How the Court case go? Steven get away?

MERTEL: No. Two years him get. Me just see you two boy picny them, say them a dead fe hungry, and me must tell you say them soon come for them dinner.

MAMMA D: Come home for them dinner yes. Me sorry to hear 'bout Steven, though, Mertel. Me must go and turn down the fire under that pot before them boy food burn up.

MERTEL: It might teach Steven the lesson him need, yaa, Mamma D. You put out plates for four, though? Expectin' John?

MAMMA D: Lord! Me forget. Me don't even 'member puttin' them out. (*They stand, going to walk off to the right of the room.*)

MERTEL: Never mind that now. You mean say you been dreamin' all this time? A two hours ago me lef' ya, you know. It's a wonder fe true say you dinner don't burn up. (*They are walking off.*)
You must tell me all about dis dream.

MAMMA D: Well, it start off in the . . .
(*They exit.*)
(*Blackout.*)